CHESTER & CHUN LING

Will D. Campbell
illustrated by Jim Hsieh

Abingdon Press
Nashville

Chester and Chun Ling

Library of Congress Cataloging-in-Publication Data

Campbell, Will D.
  Chester and Chun Ling/ Will Campbell; illustrated by Jim Hsieh.

     p. cm.
  Summary: A guitar and a violin accept their love for one another, despite differences in their appearance and the kinds of music they make.

  ISBN 0-687-06481-3

  [1. Guitar—Fiction. 2. Violin—Fiction. 3. Musical instruments—Fiction. 4. Prejudices—Fiction.]   I. Hsieh, Jim, ill.
  II. Title
  PZ7.C1613Ch 1989   88-7398
  [E]—dc19   CIP
                                                                              AC

Manufactured in Singapore

For Yobi

Chester the guitar and Chun Ling the violin sat high up on a shelf, side by side, in the Good Sound Music Store on Melody Street. They had been there many months and were very lonely. They had new strings and wanted to make pretty music. But no one ever asked to look at them, asked to hold them.

They were quiet most of the time. Except when they talked to each other. They weren't as lonely when they talked to each other.

Chester the guitar knew that they liked each other very much. But he thought they were just good friends. He had never thought of marrying Chun Ling. He had never thought of marrying anyone. Not an orphan in a music store anyway. Maybe some day. Some day when a nice family adopted him and he was out of there.

But one day Chun Ling just came right out and asked him, "Will you marry me?" Her words sort of rang a bell. Or struck a chord. Or something. Chester felt funny. Like when someone tosses you in the air and you're coming down real fast. Or riding down a steep hill on a snow sled.

Then he thought, "Big flat-top guitars are tough and frolicsome and aren't supposed to feel this way. Violins are supposed to be sad and sentimental and can feel that way when they feel that way. But not guitars." Or that's what he had been told. Since that was what he had been told, that's what he thought.

He had also been told that big, tough guitars weren't supposed to be embarrassed either. And he thought that too.

So, thinking the way someone had told him to think, he just got mad. He got huffy, crazy, rabid, raving mad! Except he was just pretending. Actually he was what someone had told him he shouldn't be; he was embarrassed. So he yelled, "I wouldn't marry you if you were the last fiddle in the world!"

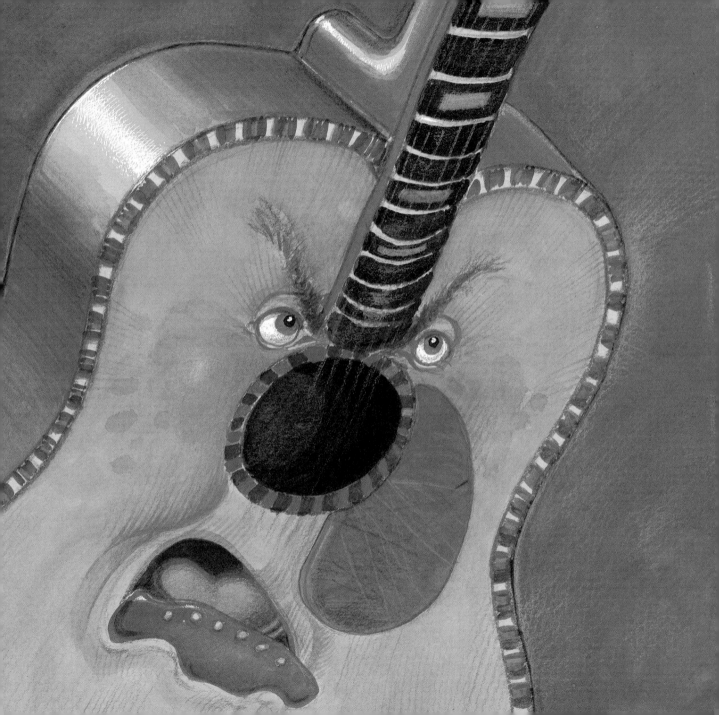

"But I'm not a fiddle," Chun Ling said, smiling and blinking her big dark eyes with long lashes. "I'm a violin."

"Well, fiddle dee dee, violin. I still wouldn't marry you," he snorted.

"Why?'

"Because. That's why."

"Because what?"

"Just because!"

"Just because what?" She was still speaking softly. And still smiling.

"Because . . . because . . . because!!!" He yelled it with a high C chord, the most shrill chord on his neck.

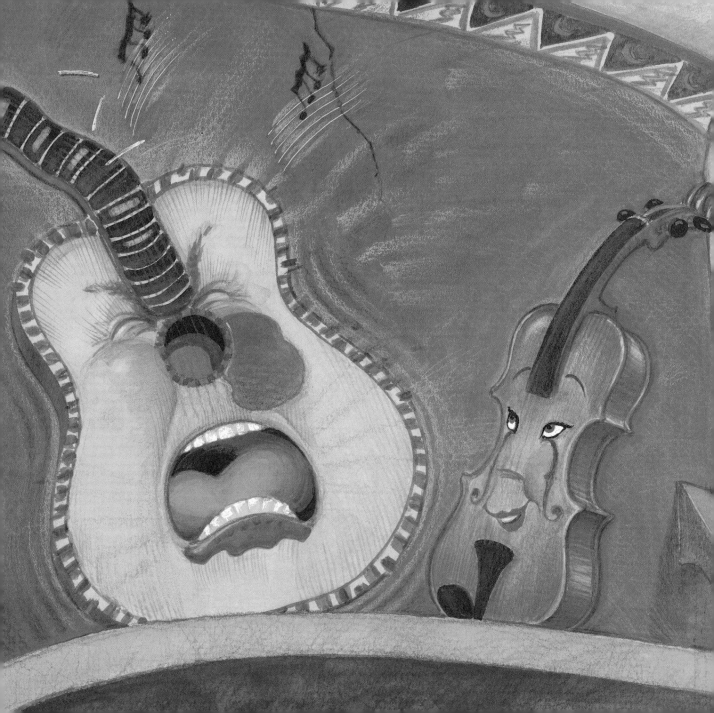

"Oh, I see. Because . . . because . . . because. Now that's a nice reason. At least I suppose it is. I hadn't thought of because . . . because . . . because. Not between friends like us."

Chun Ling knew that he wasn't actually mad, that he was just embarrassed. She didn't want to hurt his feelings. But she wasn't going to let him get away with stuff and nonsense either.

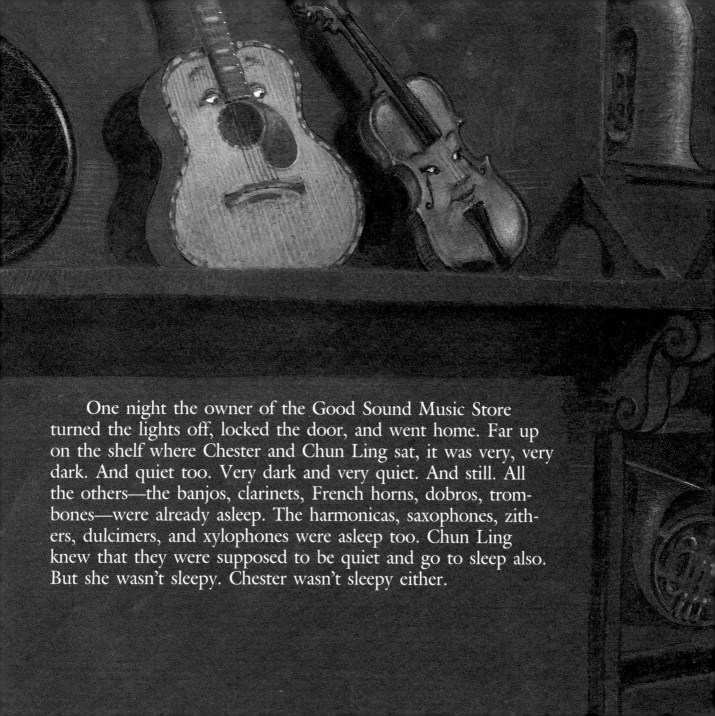

One night the owner of the Good Sound Music Store turned the lights off, locked the door, and went home. Far up on the shelf where Chester and Chun Ling sat, it was very, very dark. And quiet too. Very dark and very quiet. And still. All the others—the banjos, clarinets, French horns, dobros, trombones—were already asleep. The harmonicas, saxophones, zithers, dulcimers, and xylophones were asleep too. Chun Ling knew that they were supposed to be quiet and go to sleep also. But she wasn't sleepy. Chester wasn't sleepy either.

Both of them were quiet for a long, long time. But they weren't asleep. Just quiet. And still. With deep dark all around them. Deep, deep dark.

Chun Ling spoke first. "Chester?" She whispered it.

"What?"

"Will you marry me?"

"Uh . . . uh . . . no. I think I'd better not." There was a whiffling in his voice.

"Why? I mean *really* why this time. Not because . . . because . . . because."

"Well, you don't look like me for one thing," he said, dropping to a lower chord.

Chun Ling laughed and laughed and laughed. "Swing, zing, twang, zwing, twing, he-he-he-he-oh-ho-ho, zwang ho. Of course, I don't look like you. Would you want to marry someone who looked like you?"

Chun Ling could tell that he wasn't embarrassed any longer. And he wasn't pretending to be mad either. He was thinking for himself now. Not thinking hard yet. But thinking. "But I'm a guitar and you're a fiddle," he said. "Guitars are cowboys, and fiddles are . . . well, a nice fiddle like you just shouldn't marry a guitar like me. Hasn't anybody told you that?"

He sounded sad. Not like he had sounded before. Chun Ling thought he was going to cry, so she decided to try to make him laugh. "Guitar, sitar, kitar, charango, chitarino, ukulele! And high diddle diddle, the cat and the fiddle, and milk was the highest when the cow jumped over the moon." Then she added, "Anyway, I'm not a fiddle. I'm a violin."

Neither of them said anything for a long time again. Finally Chester whispered, "Chun Ling?" He spoke gently. Like a flower speaking.

"I am right here, Chester," she answered from the darkness. He felt her nudge closer to his side of the shelf.

"Chun Ling, I know you are a violin." His voice was soft. "But you must understand and not be angry when I call you a fiddle. I'm a big cowboy guitar. We play stout songs about trucks and trains and homes on the range. We are boisterous and loud. You make sweet tender sounds for delicate ears; you play symphonies for elegant folk."

"There is something you must understand too, Chester," she said. "It really doesn't bother me when you call me a fiddle. For sometimes I am a fiddle. Sometimes we do play satin symphonies, but sometimes we play wild breakdowns and blustery hootenannies. It depends on who is holding us, on who is our master. And that is true of you as well."

Chester answered with a clear and pleasant C chord. Then in slow succession he added A minor, D minor, G, C. The chords were the beginning of an Elvis Presley song. Delicate but brave.

"I love you, Chester," Chun Ling the violin played with true tenderness.

"Why didn't you say that in the beginning?" Chester played back.

"I did. I asked you to marry me. Isn't that the same thing?"

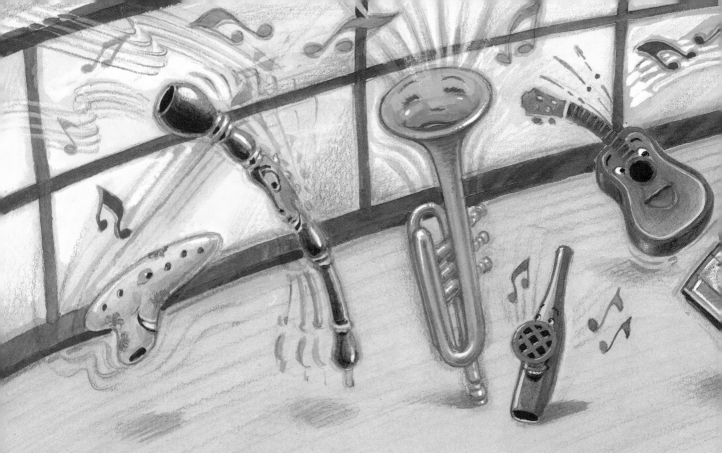

It was a melodious occasion, that wedding. Everyone was happy, including the handsome bassoon who was the preacher. The bass fiddle was the groomsman, the viola maid of honor. The oboe was a funny sight dancing with the ocarina. The kazoo and the trumpet did a duet. The bagpipe played a solo, while the uke and the autoharp did Scottish jigs.

Everyone acted delightfully silly, just having a good time.

But they all grew quiet and serious when Chester and Chun Ling began a song together, a song no one had ever heard before. It lasted far into the night. Even to this day they make glorious music together.

Sometimes, late at night, when it is very dark, still and quiet in your room and everyone else is asleep, maybe you can hear them.